The Cake That Mack Ate

To Darrell
He takes the cake

Little, Brown and Company

Hachette Book Group
237 Park Avenue, New York, NY 10017
Visit our website at www.lb-kids.com

Little, Brown and Company is a division of
Hachette Book Group, Inc.
The Little, Brown name and logo are trademarks of
Hachette Book Group, Inc.

The publisher is not responsible for websites (or their content)
that are not owned by the publisher.

First U.S. Paperback Edition: September 1991
First U.S. Hardcover Edition: April 1987

First Published in Canada by Kids Can Press

ISBN 978-0-316-74890-2 (hc) / ISBN 978-0-316-74891-9 (pb)

Library of Congress Catalog Card Number 86–47709
Library of Congress Cataloging-in-Publication
information is available.

20

Printed by Everbest Printing Co. Ltd., in China

The Cake That Mack Ate

WRITTEN BY Rose Robart
ILLUSTRATED BY Maryann Kovalski

L B
LITTLE, BROWN AND COMPANY
New York Boston

This is the cake
that Mack ate.

This is the egg
That went into the cake
that Mack ate.

This is the hen
That laid the egg,
That went into the cake
   that Mack ate.

This is the corn
That fed the hen,
That laid the egg,
That went into the cake
that Mack ate.

This is the seed
That grew into corn,
That fed the hen,
That laid the egg,
That went into the cake
that Mack ate.

This is the farmer
Who planted the seed,
That grew into corn,
That fed the hen,
That laid the egg,
That went into the cake
that Mack ate.

This is the woman
Who married the farmer,
Who planted the seed,
That grew into corn,
That fed the hen,
That laid the egg,
That went into the cake
    that Mack ate.

These are the candles
That lit up the cake,
That was made by the woman,
Who married the farmer,
Who planted the seed,
That grew into corn,
That fed the hen,
That laid the egg,
That went into the cake
    that Mack ate.

This is Mack . . .

He ate the cake.